KUNG FU PANDA 2™

MAD LIBS®

concept created by Roger Price & Leonard Stern

PSS!
PRICE STERN SLOAN
An Imprint of Penguin Group (USA) Inc.

PRICE STERN SLOAN
Published by the Penguin Group
Penguin Group (USA) Inc., 375 Hudson Street, New York, New York 10014, USA
Penguin Group (Canada), 90 Eglinton Avenue East, Suite 700,
Toronto, Ontario M4P 2Y3, Canada
(a division of Pearson Penguin Canada Inc.)
Penguin Books Ltd., 80 Strand, London WC2R 0RL, England
Penguin Group Ireland, 25 St. Stephen's Green, Dublin 2, Ireland
(a division of Penguin Books Ltd.)
Penguin Group (Australia), 250 Camberwell Road, Camberwell, Victoria 3124, Australia
(a division of Pearson Australia Group Pty. Ltd.)
Penguin Books India Pvt. Ltd., 11 Community Centre,
Panchsheel Park, New Delhi—110 017, India
Penguin Group (NZ), 67 Apollo Drive, Rosedale, North Shore 0632, New Zealand
(a division of Pearson New Zealand Ltd.)
Penguin Books (South Africa) (Pty.) Ltd., 24 Sturdee Avenue,
Rosebank, Johannesburg 2196, South Africa

Penguin Books Ltd., Registered Offices:
80 Strand, London WC2R 0RL, England

MAD LIBS®

INSTRUCTIONS

MAD LIBS® is a game for people who don't like games!
It can be played by one, two, three, four, or forty.

● RIDICULOUSLY SIMPLE DIRECTIONS

In this tablet you will find stories containing blank spaces where words are left out. One player, the **READER**, selects one of these stories. The **READER** does not tell anyone what the story is about. Instead, he/she asks the other players, the **WRITERS**, to give him/her words. These words are used to fill in the blank spaces in the story.

● TO PLAY

The **READER** asks each **WRITER** in turn to call out words—an adjective or a noun or whatever the space calls for—and uses them to fill in the blank spaces in the story. The result is a **MAD LIBS**® game.

When the **READER** then reads the completed **MAD LIBS**® game to the other players, they will discover that they have written a story that is fantastic, screamingly funny, shocking, silly, crazy, or just plain dumb—depending upon which words each **WRITER** called out.

● EXAMPLE (*Before* and *After*)

"_____!" he said _____
    EXCLAMATION   ADVERB

as he jumped into his convertible _____ and
                                       NOUN

drove off with his _____ wife.
                  ADJECTIVE

"_____*Ouch*_____!" he said _____*stupidly*_____
    EXCLAMATION   ADVERB

as he jumped into his convertible _____*cat*_____ and
                                   NOUN

drove off with his _____*brave*_____ wife.
                  ADJECTIVE

MAD LIBS®

QUICK REVIEW

In case you have forgotten what adjectives, adverbs, nouns, and verbs are, here is a quick review:

An **ADJECTIVE** describes something or somebody. *Lumpy, soft, ugly, messy,* and *short* are adjectives.

An **ADVERB** tells how something is done. It modifies a verb and usually ends in "ly." *Modestly, stupidly, greedily,* and *carefully* are adverbs.

A **NOUN** is the name of a person, place, or thing. *Sidewalk, umbrella, bridle, bathtub,* and *nose* are nouns.

A **VERB** is an action word. *Run, pitch, jump,* and *swim* are verbs. Put the verbs in past tense if the directions say PAST TENSE. *Ran, pitched, jumped,* and *swam* are verbs in the past tense.

When we ask for **A PLACE**, we mean any sort of place: a country or city *(Spain, Cleveland)* or a room *(bathroom, kitchen).*

An **EXCLAMATION** or **SILLY WORD** is any sort of funny sound, gasp, grunt, or outcry, like *Wow!, Ouch!, Whomp!, Ick!,* and *Gadzooks!*

When we ask for specific words, like a **NUMBER**, a **COLOR**, an **ANIMAL**, or a **PART OF THE BODY**, we mean a word that is one of those things, like *seven, blue, horse,* or *head.*

When we ask for a **PLURAL**, it means more than one. For example, *cat* pluralized is *cats.*

MAD LIBS® is fun to play with friends, but you can also play it by yourself! To begin with, DO NOT look at the story on the page below. Fill in the blanks on this page with the words called for. Then, using the words you have selected, fill in the blank spaces in the story.

Now you've created your own hilarious MAD LIBS® game!

THE EXILE FILES, BY SHEN

PLURAL NOUN _____

ADJECTIVE _____

ADJECTIVE _____

PLURAL NOUN _____

ADJECTIVE _____

NOUN _____

NOUN _____

PLURAL NOUN _____

PLURAL NOUN _____

CELEBRITY_____

PLURAL NOUN _____

ADVERB _____

PLURAL NOUN _____

ADJECTIVE _____

NOUN _____

VERB _____

MAD LIBS®

THE EXILE FILES, BY SHEN

Many ___**People**___ have risen and set in the sky since I was
    PLURAL NOUN

forced into exile. So much time has passed that it feels like I've

traveled all the way across this ___**Ugly**___ world and back
                                    ADJECTIVE

again. My heart has grown ___**Fat**___ from sorrow and
                            ADJECTIVE

anger. How could my own loving ___**Cats**___ make me leave
                                  PLURAL NOUN

my ___**Chunky**___ ancestral home? Why would they cast me
      ADJECTIVE

out like a common ___**Pig**___? They say it was for my own
                      NOUN

safety, but *I* am the rightful ___**Chicken**___ of Gongmen City—not
                                  NOUN

those three ridiculous ___**Dogs**___ that my parents named
                          PLURAL NOUN

as their successors. It is *my* destiny to rule Gongmen City and all

the ___**Hippos**___ who live there! As ___**LebronJ**___ is my
      PLURAL NOUN   CELEBRITY

witness, I swear it shall be mine one day! The army of wolves and

___**B-ball Players**___ I've recruited are ready to fight ___**sadly**___
      PLURAL NOUN   ADVERB

alongside me. With their sharp ___**Hotdogs**___ and nasty tempers,
                                  PLURAL NOUN

they are proving to be a truly ___**funny**___ army. With their help
                                 ADJECTIVE

I will reclaim my ___**Pig**___—or ___**Fast**___ trying!
                     NOUN   VERB

From KUNG FU PANDA 2 MAD LIBS® · Kung Fu Panda 2 ™ & © 2011 DreamWorks Animation L.L.C.
Kung Fu Panda ® DreamWorks Animation L.L.C. Published by Price Stern Sloan,
a division of Penguin Group (USA) Inc., 345 Hudson Street, New York, NY 10014.

MAD LIBS® is fun to play with friends, but you can also play it by yourself! To begin with, DO NOT look at the story on the page below. Fill in the blanks on this page with the words called for. Then, using the words you have selected, fill in the blank spaces in the story.

Now you've created your own hilarious MAD LIBS® game!

SOOTHSAYERS WANTED

PART OF THE BODY (PLURAL) _____

PLURAL NOUN _____

ADJECTIVE _____

TYPE OF LIQUID _____

TYPE OF FOOD _____

VERB ENDING IN "ING" _____

ADJECTIVE _____

PLURAL NOUN _____

A PLACE _____

CELEBRITY _____

PERSON IN ROOM _____

ADJECTIVE _____

PLURAL NOUN _____

PART OF THE BODY _____

ADJECTIVE _____

VERB _____

MAD LIBS®
SOOTHSAYERS WANTED

Are you good at reading _____**Toes**_____? Can you foretell
PART OF THE BODY (PLURAL)

the future using only _____**Crocs**_____? Do you see ____**Purple**____
PLURAL NOUN   ADJECTIVE

visions when you mix _____**Pepsi**_____ with powdered
TYPE OF LIQUID

_____**bananana**_____? If so, Soothsayers' Syndicate would like to hear
TYPE OF FOOD

from you! We are an exclusive group of fortune-_____**running**_____
VERB ENDING IN "ING"

experts who provide _____**Pretty**_____ services to powerful ruling

_____**Flies**_____ all over (the) _____**Egypt**_____! Satisfied clients
PLURAL NOUN   A PLACE

include _____**Brittney.S**_____ and _____**Jacob**_____. Experience is
CELEBRITY   PERSON IN ROOM

not required, but we do look for candidates who are intelligent,

patient, and _____**Skinny**_____. Priority consideration will be
ADJECTIVE

given to those with their own crystal _____**sausages**_____ If you
PLURAL NOUN

have a/an _____**thumb**_____ toward a better tomorrow, then this
PART OF THE BODY

_____**Pigish**_____ job might be right for you. _____**hop**_____
ADJECTIVE   VERB

today for an application!

From KUNG FU PANDA 2 MAD LIBS® · Kung Fu Panda 2 ™ & © 2011 DreamWorks Animation L.L.C.
Kung Fu Panda ® DreamWorks Animation L.L.C. Published by Price Stern Sloan,
a division of Penguin Group (USA) Inc., 345 Hudson Street, New York, NY 10014.

MAD LIBS® is fun to play with friends, but you can also play it by yourself! To begin with, DO NOT look at the story on the page below. Fill in the blanks on this page with the words called for. Then, using the words you have selected, fill in the blank spaces in the story.

Now you've created your own hilarious MAD LIBS® game!

YUMMY IN YOUR TUMMY!

PLURAL NOUN _____

PART OF THE BODY (PLURAL) _____

ADJECTIVE _____

NOUN _____

PLURAL NOUN _____

A PLACE _____

PLURAL NOUN _____

ADJECTIVE _____

PERSON IN ROOM (MALE) _____

ADJECTIVE _____

NOUN _____

TYPE OF FOOD _____

ARTICLE OF CLOTHING _____

ADJECTIVE _____

PART OF THE BODY _____

MAD LIBS®
YUMMY IN YOUR TUMMY!

What's that noise? It's the sound of satisfied __Peoples__
PLURAL NOUN

smacking their __Butt__ together after a/an
PART OF THE BODY (PLURAL)

__Purple__ meal at Dragon Warrior Noodles and Tofu.
ADJECTIVE

Owned and operated by longtime proprietor Mr. Ping, this

five-__chicken__ restaurant serves some of the best
NOUN

__Pigs__ in (the) __France__ ! The signature dishes
PLURAL NOUN   A PLACE

include creamed __Flics__ over noodles with crispy,
PLURAL NOUN

__Pink__ tofu fries. The place was also home to the famed
ADJECTIVE

Dragon Warrior, __Trinton__ . That's right—if you want
PERSON IN ROOM (MALE)

a look at the early life of that __Ugly__ kung fu panda,
ADJECTIVE

look no further. The walls are covered with memorabilia such

as the __Isaac__ he used to mop the floors and the
NOUN

__Banana__ -stained __scarf__ he wore when
TYPE OF FOOD   ARTICLE OF CLOTHING

serving customers. Come hungry—leave __Green__ . Your
ADJECTIVE

__Arm__ will thank you!
PART OF THE BODY

From KUNG FU PANDA 2 MAD LIBS® · Kung Fu Panda 2 ™ & © 2011 DreamWorks Animation L.L.C.
Kung Fu Panda ® DreamWorks Animation L.L.C. Published by Price Stern Sloan,
a division of Penguin Group (USA) Inc., 345 Hudson Street, New York, NY 10014.

MAD LIBS® is fun to play with friends, but you can also play it by yourself! To begin with, DO NOT look at the story on the page below. Fill in the blanks on this page with the words called for. Then, using the words you have selected, fill in the blank spaces in the story.

Now you've created your own hilarious MAD LIBS® game!

A DESTINY FULFILLED

PLURAL NOUN _____

NOUN _____

VERB ENDING IN "ING" _____

PLURAL NOUN _____

PART OF THE BODY _____

PLURAL NOUN _____

SILLY WORD _____

PLURAL NOUN _____

PART OF THE BODY _____

ADJECTIVE _____

PLURAL NOUN _____

ADJECTIVE _____

NOUN _____

ADJECTIVE _____

MAD LIBS

A DESTINY FULFILLED

In a million ___Farts___, Po never would have guessed how
PLURAL NOUN

much his life would change when he became the ___butthead___
NOUN

Warrior. Now whenever he goes anywhere in the Valley of Peace,

people start cheering and ___pooping___ like crazy. They
VERB ENDING IN "ING"

run right in front of speeding ___sticks___ just to shake Po's
PLURAL NOUN

___Penis___. Parents thrust their newborn ___Father___
PART OF THE BODY   _PLURAL NOUN_

into Po's arms and yell, "Say '___old man___'!" so they can
SILLY WORD

snap a photo. Kids are constantly asking him to autograph their

___boobs___. Sometimes people even try to yank a tuft of hair
PLURAL NOUN

from Po's ___butt___. Oh well. Such is the ___green___
PART OF THE BODY   _ADJECTIVE_

price of fame. As long as he still gets to battle evil ___shoes___
PLURAL NOUN

and ___pink___ villains using his beloved kung fu, Po
ADJECTIVE

takes it with a grain of ___bed___. Although having his own
NOUN

___bird___ action figure would be a pretty awesome thing, too.
ADJECTIVE

From KUNG FU PANDA 2 MAD LIBS® · Kung Fu Panda 2 ™ & © 2011 DreamWorks Animation L.L.C.
Kung Fu Panda ® DreamWorks Animation L.L.C. Published by Price Stern Sloan,
a division of Penguin Group (USA) Inc., 345 Hudson Street, New York, NY 10014.

MAD LIBS® is fun to play with friends, but you can also play it by yourself! To begin with, DO NOT look at the story on the page below. Fill in the blanks on this page with the words called for. Then, using the words you have selected, fill in the blank spaces in the story.

Now you've created your own hilarious MAD LIBS® game!

BABY PO

NOUN _____

NOUN _____

VERB (PAST TENSE) _____

EXCLAMATION _____

NOUN _____

ADJECTIVE _____

NOUN _____

ARTICLE OF CLOTHING (PLURAL) _____

VERB ENDING IN "ING"_____

PART OF THE BODY (PLURAL) _____

ADJECTIVE _____

ADJECTIVE _____

NOUN _____

NOUN _____

MAD LIBS
BABY PO

Soon after finding Po hidden in a/an _____ basket

NOUN

with his morning vegetable delivery, Mr. Ping realized this little

_____ was different. Sure, he slept and _____

NOUN   VERB (PAST TENSE)

all day like most babies—but _____—that little

EXCLAMATION

panda could eat! It was like he had a bottomless _____

NOUN

for a stomach! In fact, there were many days that Mr. Ping feared

his _____ son would eat him out of house and

ADJECTIVE

_____. But as much as Po liked eating, he *disliked*

NOUN

wearing _____. In fact, whenever Mr. Ping

ARTICLE OF CLOTHING (PLURAL)

tried to get him dressed, Po would take off _____

VERB ENDING IN "ING"

as fast as his chubby _____ could carry him. Then

PART OF THE BODY (PLURAL)

one day Mr. Ping had a/an _____ idea. He discovered

ADJECTIVE

that when he left a trail of _____ dumplings or

ADJECTIVE

_____-covered tofu balls, he could get Po to do whatever

NOUN

he wanted: get in the bath, take a nap, or just lie still long enough for

Mr. Ping to change his dirty _____!

NOUN

MAD LIBS® is fun to play with friends, but you can also play it by yourself! To begin with, DO NOT look at the story on the page below. Fill in the blanks on this page with the words called for. Then, using the words you have selected, fill in the blank spaces in the story.

Now you've created your own hilarious MAD LIBS® game!

(ACTION) FIGURES
OF AWESOMENESS

ADJECTIVE _____

NOUN _____

PLURAL NOUN _____

ADJECTIVE _____

VERB ENDING IN "ING" _____

PLURAL NOUN _____

PERSON IN ROOM _____

ADJECTIVE _____

PART OF THE BODY (PLURAL) _____

ADJECTIVE _____

PERSON IN ROOM (MALE) _____

PLURAL NOUN _____

ADVERB _____

NOUN _____

NUMBER _____

VERB _____

NOUN _____

MAD LIBS®
(ACTION) FIGURES
OF AWESOMENESS

Are you a fan of kung fu? Do you worship the _____

ADJECTIVE

team known as the _____ Warrior and the Furious

NOUN

_____? Do you wish you could be as awesomely

PLURAL NOUN

_____ as they are? Well, you can't—but you *could* be the

ADJECTIVE

proud owner of a limited-edition action figure collection of these

kung fu _____ heroes. Handcrafted from the finest

VERB ENDING IN "ING"

_____ by world-famous designer _____, these

PLURAL NOUN   PERSON IN ROOM

_____ figures feature movable _____

ADJECTIVE   PART OF THE BODY (PLURAL)

that you can bend into _____ kung fu poses. Re-create

ADJECTIVE

famous battle scenes, like when the Furious Five defeated the

evil Lord _____ and his army of _____.

PERSON IN ROOM (MALE)   PLURAL NOUN

Or _____ display them on a/an _____ in

ADVERB   NOUN

your room. This collection can be yours for only six installments

of _____ dollars. If you _____ now we'll also

NUMBER   VERB

send you a bonus Master Shifu figure. After all, no team is complete

without its fearless _____!

NOUN

From KUNG FU PANDA 2 MAD LIBS® · Kung Fu Panda 2 ™ & © 2011 DreamWorks Animation L.L.C.
Kung Fu Panda ® DreamWorks Animation L.L.C. Published by Price Stern Sloan,
a division of Penguin Group (USA) Inc., 345 Hudson Street, New York, NY 10014.

MAD LIBS® is fun to play with friends, but you can also play it by yourself! To begin with, DO NOT look at the story on the page below. Fill in the blanks on this page with the words called for. Then, using the words you have selected, fill in the blank spaces in the story.

Now you've created your own hilarious MAD LIBS® game!

AWESOME KUNG FU MOVES

NOUN _____

NUMBER _____

A PLACE _____

ADJECTIVE _____

PART OF THE BODY (PLURAL) _____

PERSON IN ROOM _____

ADVERB _____

NOUN _____

NOUN _____

PERSON IN ROOM _____

PLURAL NOUN _____

PART OF THE BODY (PLURAL) _____

ADJECTIVE _____

PLURAL NOUN _____

PERSON IN ROOM _____

PART OF THE BODY (PLURAL) _____

MAD LIBS
AWESOME KUNG FU MOVES

The _____ Warrior and the Furious _____ are
      NOUN   NUMBER

admired all over (the) _____ for their _____
                       A PLACE   ADJECTIVE

kung fu techniques, including these signature moves:

• _____ of Justice: _____ swoops in,
  PART OF THE BODY (PLURAL)   PERSON IN ROOM

grabs Po as he is _____ diving in midair, and hurls him
                  ADVERB

forward faster than a speeding _____.
                               NOUN

• Double-_____ Strike: Tigress whirls _____
         NOUN   PERSON IN ROOM

around like a windmill, sending _____ flying in
                                PLURAL NOUN

every direction.

• Feet of Fury: Po moves his _____ so quickly
                             PART OF THE BODY (PLURAL)

that the _____ enemies look like _____
         ADJECTIVE   PLURAL NOUN

raining down from the sky.

• Hard Style: Favored by _____, this extreme style of
                         PERSON IN ROOM

kung fu is practiced by those who train until no feeling remains in

their _____.
      PART OF THE BODY (PLURAL)

MAD LIBS® is fun to play with friends, but you can also play it by yourself! To begin with, DO NOT look at the story on the page below. Fill in the blanks on this page with the words called for. Then, using the words you have selected, fill in the blank spaces in the story.

Now you've created your own hilarious MAD LIBS® game!

PEACOCK DYNASTY

ADJECTIVE _____

NOUN _____

ADJECTIVE _____

PLURAL NOUN _____

PLURAL NOUN _____

ADJECTIVE _____

PLURAL NOUN _____

PLURAL NOUN _____

NOUN _____

PERSON IN ROOM (MALE) _____

ADJECTIVE _____

PLURAL NOUN _____

PART OF THE BODY (PLURAL) _____

ADJECTIVE _____

COLOR _____

ADJECTIVE _____

MAD LIBS®
PEACOCK DYNASTY

Gongmen City was once a safe and thriving metropolis. But when

the vindictive and _____ Lord Shen returned to Gongmen
ADJECTIVE

City and proclaimed it the Year of the _____, life took
NOUN

a turn for the _____ for the good _____
ADJECTIVE   PLURAL NOUN

who lived there. Chaos and destructive _____ ran
PLURAL NOUN

rampant through the city. Shen's _____ army
ADJECTIVE

terrorized the citizens, stealing all their metal _____
PLURAL NOUN

to use at the cannon factory. The people lived in fear for their

_____. _____-wielding guards forced them
PLURAL NOUN   NOUN

to chant "Hail to _____, His Royal _____-
PERSON IN ROOM (MALE)   ADJECTIVE

ness!" whenever Shen walked by. The loyal _____ of
PLURAL NOUN

Gongmen City could only cross their _____ and
PART OF THE BODY (PLURAL)

hope that the ancient prophecy was true: a/an _____
ADJECTIVE

warrior of black and _____ would one day restore
COLOR

Gongmen City to the gloriously _____ kingdom it once was.
ADJECTIVE

From KUNG FU PANDA 2 MAD LIBS® · Kung Fu Panda 2 ™ & © 2011 DreamWorks Animation L.L.C.
Kung Fu Panda ® DreamWorks Animation L.L.C. Published by Price Stern Sloan,
a division of Penguin Group (USA) Inc., 345 Hudson Street, New York, NY 10014.

MAD LIBS® is fun to play with friends, but you can also play it by yourself! To begin with, DO NOT look at the story on the page below. Fill in the blanks on this page with the words called for. Then, using the words you have selected, fill in the blank spaces in the story.

Now you've created your own hilarious MAD LIBS® game!

THE BATTLE
AT THE CANNON FACTORY

NOUN _____

ADJECTIVE _____

A PLACE _____

PLURAL NOUN _____

NOUN _____

PERSON IN ROOM (MALE) _____

NOUN _____

PART OF THE BODY _____

PLURAL NOUN _____

TYPE OF LIQUID _____

NOUN _____

PART OF THE BODY _____

ADJECTIVE _____

PART OF THE BODY (PLURAL) _____

ADJECTIVE _____

VERB _____

MAD LIBS
THE BATTLE
AT THE CANNON FACTORY

Po headed to the _____ factory to destroy Shen's

NOUN

weapons and thwart his _____ plan to take over (the)

ADJECTIVE

_____. He sneaked past armed _____ and

A PLACE   PLURAL NOUN

vaulted up the scaffolding. A peacock-shaped _____

NOUN

emerged from the shadows—it was _____! He

PERSON IN ROOM (MALE)

pulled a lever and a/an _____ swung out, nearly

NOUN

knocking Po off. But Po hung on and charged Shen. Shen kicked

Po right in the _____, and Po tumbled onto a conveyor

PART OF THE BODY

belt full of scrap-metal _____. The panda was about

PLURAL NOUN

to be dumped into a vat of scalding _____ when

TYPE OF LIQUID

he grabbed a/an _____ and thrust it into the conveyor

NOUN

belt, saving his _____! Po went after Shen again, but

PART OF THE BODY

Shen lit a/an _____ cannon and blew Po head over

ADJECTIVE

_____ right through the building. Was this

PART OF THE BODY (PLURAL)

the end for our _____ hero? Or would he live to

ADJECTIVE

_____ another day?

VERB

From KUNG FU PANDA 2 MAD LIBS® · Kung Fu Panda 2 ™ & © 2011 DreamWorks Animation L.L.C.
Kung Fu Panda ® DreamWorks Animation L.L.C. Published by Price Stern Sloan,
a division of Penguin Group (USA) Inc., 345 Hudson Street, New York, NY 10014.

MAD LIBS® is fun to play with friends, but you can also play it by yourself! To begin with, DO NOT look at the story on the page below. Fill in the blanks on this page with the words called for. Then, using the words you have selected, fill in the blank spaces in the story.

Now you've created your own hilarious MAD LIBS® game!

RICKSHAW DRIVER'S ED

NOUN _____

ADJECTIVE _____

PART OF THE BODY (PLURAL) _____

ADJECTIVE _____

ADJECTIVE _____

PLURAL NOUN _____

PLURAL NOUN _____

ADJECTIVE _____

VERB ENDING IN "ING" _____

ADJECTIVE _____

PLURAL NOUN _____

TYPE OF LIQUID _____

ADJECTIVE _____

TYPE OF LIQUID _____

NOUN _____

PART OF THE BODY (PLURAL) _____

MAD LIBS
RICKSHAW DRIVER'S ED

Not every _____ can drive a rickshaw. It takes someone with
                  NOUN

_____ _____ and a/an _____
   ADJECTIVE   PART OF THE BODY (PLURAL)   ADJECTIVE

sense of balance. To ensure a safe and _____ rickshaw
                                              ADJECTIVE

driving experience, follow these rules of the road.

1. Make sure your _____ are buckled in so they don't fly
                      PLURAL NOUN

   out at sudden stops.

2. Keep in mind that _____ always have the right of way,
                        PLURAL NOUN

   so be extra _____ when approaching a crosswalk.
                   ADJECTIVE

3. It's important to keep a rickshaw in good _____
                                               VERB ENDING IN "ING"

   order. Perform all the _____ maintenance required by
                              ADJECTIVE

   the owner's manual, such as keeping the _____ fully
                                               PLURAL NOUN

   inflated and lubricated with premium _____.
                                           TYPE OF LIQUID

4. Remember that rickshaws don't run on _____
                                                ADJECTIVE

   unleaded _____. The _____ is supplied
               TYPE OF LIQUID   NOUN

   by the power of your _____, so be sure to keep
                          PART OF THE BODY (PLURAL)

   them in good shape!

From KUNG FU PANDA 2 MAD LIBS® · Kung Fu Panda 2 ™ & © 2011 DreamWorks Animation L.L.C.
Kung Fu Panda ® DreamWorks Animation L.L.C. Published by Price Stern Sloan,
a division of Penguin Group (USA) Inc., 345 Hudson Street, New York, NY 10014.

MAD LIBS® is fun to play with friends, but you can also play it by yourself! To begin with, DO NOT look at the story on the page below. Fill in the blanks on this page with the words called for. Then, using the words you have selected, fill in the blank spaces in the story.

Now you've created your own hilarious MAD LIBS® game!

MR. PING SENDS PO PACKING

ADJECTIVE _____

NOUN _____

ADJECTIVE _____

NOUN _____

PERSON IN ROOM _____

PART OF THE BODY (PLURAL) _____

PLURAL NOUN _____

NOUN _____

ADJECTIVE _____

PLURAL NOUN _____

TYPE OF LIQUID _____

NOUN _____

ADJECTIVE _____

ADJECTIVE _____

PLURAL NOUN _____

PART OF THE BODY _____

A PLACE _____

PART OF THE BODY (PLURAL) _____

MAD LIBS
MR. PING SENDS PO PACKING

Po, my _____ son: You know how much I love you.
        ADJECTIVE

You are my only _____—my _____ family!
                    NOUN   ADJECTIVE

Although I know kung fu has been a/an _____ come
                                          NOUN

true for you and that Master _____ has trained you
                              PERSON IN ROOM

well, I still wring my _____ with worry whenever
                       PART OF THE BODY (PLURAL)

you must fight evil _____. Please take care of yourself,
                     PLURAL NOUN

dear Po. I have packed you plenty of food—_____ chip
                                              NOUN

cookies, _____ bean buns, tofu _____,
          ADJECTIVE   PLURAL NOUN

and canteens of _____. I also packed your favorite
                 TYPE OF LIQUID

stuffed _____ and your Furious Five action figures.
         NOUN

And, of course, I don't want you to be lonely or _____,
                                                  ADJECTIVE

so I packed paintings of our _____ times together
                              ADJECTIVE

cooking noodle _____ and of me giving you a
                PLURAL NOUN

piggy-_____ ride. Now go help the people of (the)
       PART OF THE BODY

_____—and when you return, I'll greet you with open
 A PLACE

_____.
 PART OF THE BODY (PLURAL)

From KUNG FU PANDA 2 MAD LIBS® · Kung Fu Panda 2 ™ & © 2011 DreamWorks Animation L.L.C.
Kung Fu Panda ® DreamWorks Animation L.L.C. Published by Price Stern Sloan,
a division of Penguin Group (USA) Inc., 345 Hudson Street, New York, NY 10014.

MAD LIBS® is fun to play with friends, but you can also play it by yourself! To begin with, DO NOT look at the story on the page below. Fill in the blanks on this page with the words called for. Then, using the words you have selected, fill in the blank spaces in the story.

Now you've created your own hilarious MAD LIBS® game!

OUR CANNONS ARE A BLAST

ADJECTIVE _____

NOUN _____

PART OF THE BODY (PLURAL) _____

VERB _____

ADJECTIVE _____

ADVERB _____

ADJECTIVE _____

PLURAL NOUN _____

ADJECTIVE _____

NOUN _____

PLURAL NOUN _____

PART OF THE BODY _____

NUMBER _____

PLURAL NOUN _____

PLURAL NOUN _____

MAD LIBS

OUR CANNONS ARE A BLAST

Looking for a/an _____ weapon to make even the greatest
                        ADJECTIVE

kung fu _____ crumble to his _____? Then
              NOUN   PART OF THE BODY (PLURAL)

look no further than the Cannon Factory! We _____
                                                VERB

hard all day and night to manufacture cannons that meet all

your _____ explosive needs. Our _____
          ADJECTIVE   ADVERB

discounted cannons come in all kinds of _____ shapes
                                              ADJECTIVE

and sizes. Crafted from the finest _____, these sleek,
                                      PLURAL NOUN

_____ barrels will launch a/an _____ at
     ADJECTIVE   NOUN

dizzying speeds. For those fashion-conscious warlords, we offer

designer patterns such as camouflage _____ and
                                          PLURAL NOUN

sculptured cannons featuring a dragon's _____. Our
                                          PART OF THE BODY

factory is open _____ day(s) a week for your convenience,
                   NUMBER

and we accept cash, checks, or _____. Satisfaction
                                   PLURAL NOUN

guaranteed—or your _____ back!
                        PLURAL NOUN

MAD LIBS® is fun to play with friends, but you can also play it by yourself! To begin with, DO NOT look at the story on the page below. Fill in the blanks on this page with the words called for. Then, using the words you have selected, fill in the blank spaces in the story.

Now you've created your own hilarious MAD LIBS® game!

FLASHBACK ATTACK

PART OF THE BODY _____

PART OF THE BODY _____

ADJECTIVE _____

PART OF THE BODY _____

TYPE OF LIQUID _____

PART OF THE BODY _____

ADJECTIVE _____

ADJECTIVE _____

NOUN _____

NOUN _____

ADJECTIVE _____

TYPE OF LIQUID _____

PLURAL NOUN _____

NOUN _____

TYPE OF LIQUID _____

ADJECTIVE _____

NOUN _____

MAD LIBS®
FLASHBACK ATTACK

Po was worried that he was inexplicably losing his

_____. The last few times he was engaged in hand-
PART OF THE BODY

to-_____ combat with Shen's wolves, he suddenly felt
PART OF THE BODY

_____-headed. There was a quivering sensation in his
ADJECTIVE

_____ and beads of _____ poured down
PART OF THE BODY   TYPE OF LIQUID

his _____. Everything in front of him got blurry and
PART OF THE BODY

_____, and Po could see nothing but an enormous,
ADJECTIVE

_____ flashing _____. Then that image
ADJECTIVE   NOUN

faded, and his mom and _____ appeared. What did
NOUN

these _____ visions mean? Po thought he was drinking
ADJECTIVE

too much green _____ or eating too many chocolate-
TYPE OF LIQUID

covered _____. He wondered if throwing some grains
PLURAL NOUN

of _____ over his left shoulder would help, or if maybe
NOUN

he should relax in a steaming tub of _____. As the
TYPE OF LIQUID

Dragon Warrior, Po knew he had to stop these _____
ADJECTIVE

distractions. It was a matter of life or _____!
NOUN

From KUNG FU PANDA 2 MAD LIBS® · Kung Fu Panda 2 ™ & © 2011 DreamWorks Animation L.L.C.
Kung Fu Panda ® DreamWorks Animation L.L.C. Published by Price Stern Sloan,
a division of Penguin Group (USA) Inc., 345 Hudson Street, New York, NY 10014.

MAD LIBS® is fun to play with friends, but you can also play it by yourself! To begin with, DO NOT look at the story on the page below. Fill in the blanks on this page with the words called for. Then, using the words you have selected, fill in the blank spaces in the story.

Now you've created your own hilarious MAD LIBS® game!

THE LEGENDARY MASTERS

VERB ENDING IN "ING" _____

NOUN _____

NOUN _____

A PLACE _____

ADJECTIVE _____

NOUN _____

ADJECTIVE _____

PERSON IN ROOM _____

NUMBER _____

PLURAL NOUN _____

PLURAL NOUN _____

ADJECTIVE _____

NUMBER _____

PLURAL NOUN _____

PART OF THE BODY (PLURAL) _____

Before they were appointed to protect Gongmen City, Masters

Rhino, Croc, and Ox were kung fu _____ legends. Here
VERB ENDING IN "ING"

are the warriors' brief bios:

• Master Thundering _____ was born on a small
NOUN

_____ off the coast of (the) _____. He is best
NOUN   A PLACE

known for single handedly annihilating a squad of _____
ADJECTIVE

assassins using only a handheld _____.
NOUN

• Master Croc came from a/an _____ family and
ADJECTIVE

trained under Grand Master _____. He stopped
PERSON IN ROOM

_____ _____ from destroying the gentle
NUMBER   PLURAL NOUN

_____ who lived on the island of Chen Wei.
PLURAL NOUN

• Master Storming Ox perfected the _____ scissors
ADJECTIVE

kick move. He is reputed to have taken out _____
NUMBER

_____ in the sinking rice fields of the Wang Chung
PLURAL NOUN

province with nothing but his bare _____.
PART OF THE BODY (PLURAL)

From KUNG FU PANDA 2 MAD LIBS® · Kung Fu Panda 2 ™ & © 2011 DreamWorks Animation L.L.C.
Kung Fu Panda ® DreamWorks Animation L.L.C. Published by Price Stern Sloan,
a division of Penguin Group (USA) Inc., 345 Hudson Street, New York, NY 10014.

MAD LIBS® is fun to play with friends, but you can also play it by yourself! To begin with, DO NOT look at the story on the page below. Fill in the blanks on this page with the words called for. Then, using the words you have selected, fill in the blank spaces in the story.

Now you've created your own hilarious MAD LIBS® game!

INNER PEACE 101, BY MASTER SHIFU

PART OF THE BODY _____

ADJECTIVE _____

PART OF THE BODY (PLURAL) _____

ADVERB _____

PART OF THE BODY (PLURAL) _____

ADJECTIVE _____

NOUN _____

ADJECTIVE _____

SILLY WORD _____

SAME SILLY WORD_____

PLURAL NOUN _____

NOUN _____

ADVERB _____

ADJECTIVE _____

PART OF THE BODY _____

NOUN _____

MAD LIBS®
INNER PEACE 101,
BY MASTER SHIFU

If you are at peace, your mind and your _____

_____
PART OF THE BODY

become one. Anyone can achieve Inner Peace by following this

_____ step-by-step guide.
ADJECTIVE

1. Close your _____ tightly and breathe in and out
   PART OF THE BODY (PLURAL)

   calmly and _____.
   ADVERB

2. Begin to move your _____ in _____,
   PART OF THE BODY (PLURAL)   ADJECTIVE

   graceful motions—almost like a winged _____ in flight.
   NOUN

3. When you have a/an _____ rhythm going, begin to
   ADJECTIVE

   chant "_____, _____" and picture
   SILLY WORD   SAME SILLY WORD

   a beautiful scene, like long-stemmed wild _____
   PLURAL NOUN

   swaying gently in a field or a/an _____ bobbing
   NOUN

   _____ on the ocean waves.
   ADVERB

When you feel a/an _____ sensation filling your
ADJECTIVE

_____, congratulations! You have officially achieved
PART OF THE BODY

Inner _____.
NOUN

From KUNG FU PANDA 2 MAD LIBS® · Kung Fu Panda 2 ™ & © 2011 DreamWorks Animation L.L.C.
Kung Fu Panda ® DreamWorks Animation L.L.C. Published by Price Stern Sloan,
a division of Penguin Group (USA) Inc., 345 Hudson Street, New York, NY 10014.

MAD LIBS® is fun to play with friends, but you can also play it by yourself! To begin with, DO NOT look at the story on the page below. Fill in the blanks on this page with the words called for. Then, using the words you have selected, fill in the blank spaces in the story.

Now you've created your own hilarious MAD LIBS® game!

ODE TO STEALTH MODE, BY PO

PART OF THE BODY _____

ADJECTIVE _____

ADJECTIVE _____

ADVERB _____

PLURAL NOUN _____

NOUN _____

VERB ENDING IN "ING" _____

ADJECTIVE _____

PART OF THE BODY (PLURAL) _____

EXCLAMATION _____

PLURAL NOUN _____

TYPE OF FOOD (PLURAL) _____

ADJECTIVE _____

ADJECTIVE _____

My _____ may be a/an _____ wide load—
  PART OF THE BODY   ADJECTIVE

but that won't stop me from trying stealth mode!

It's a cool, _____ kung fu skill:
              ADJECTIVE

I _____ sneak along—then I stay still.
    ADVERB

I dive behind _____ or maybe trees.
              PLURAL NOUN

You can hear a/an _____ drop when I freeze.
                    NOUN

_____ along on tiptoes,
VERB ENDING IN "ING"

I strike a/an _____ kung fu pose.
              ADJECTIVE

Oops! Clumsy _____! Now I've tripped!
              PART OF THE BODY (PLURAL)

_____—all the vendor carts have tipped!
EXCLAMATION

_____ and _____ crash all around—
PLURAL NOUN   TYPE OF FOOD (PLURAL)

the _____ marketplace is falling down!
    ADJECTIVE

I may be a/an _____ kung fu king,
              ADJECTIVE

but stealth mode's clearly not my thing.

MAD LIBS® is fun to play with friends, but you can also play it by yourself! To begin with, DO NOT look at the story on the page below. Fill in the blanks on this page with the words called for. Then, using the words you have selected, fill in the blank spaces in the story.

Now you've created your own hilarious MAD LIBS® game!

MASTERING THE ART OF FUN

ADJECTIVE _____

VERB _____

ADJECTIVE _____

ADJECTIVE _____

NOUN _____

PART OF THE BODY _____

PLURAL NOUN _____

PART OF THE BODY _____

PLURAL NOUN _____

PLURAL NOUN _____

ADJECTIVE _____

ADJECTIVE _____

PLURAL NOUN _____

NOUN _____

The Dragon Warrior and the Furious Five have a/an _____
ADJECTIVE

motto: Work hard, _____ harder. Here are some of the
VERB

ways they enjoy spending their _____ spare time:
ADJECTIVE

- **The Dragon Warrior:** Po spends a/an _____ amount of time
ADJECTIVE

stuffing _____ buns and dumplings into his _____.
NOUN   PART OF THE BODY

- **Tigress:** She tries to top her own record of stacking iron

_____ on top of one another and smashing them to dust
PLURAL NOUN

with one punch of her _____.
PART OF THE BODY

- **Crane and Mantis:** These two share an enthusiasm for scary

_____ in 3-D.
PLURAL NOUN

- **Viper:** She can often be found slithering around the beach

searching for metal _____ and other little, _____
PLURAL NOUN   ADJECTIVE

treasures that people have dropped.

- **Monkey:** With a passion for baking, Monkey swings through

_____ orchards, collecting ripe _____ to use
ADJECTIVE   PLURAL NOUN

in his famous _____-berry pies.
NOUN

MAD LIBS® is fun to play with friends, but you can also play it by yourself! To begin with, DO NOT look at the story on the page below. Fill in the blanks on this page with the words called for. Then, using the words you have selected, fill in the blank spaces in the story.

Now you've created your own hilarious MAD LIBS® game!

EXTREME CANNON DODGEBALL

ADJECTIVE _____

NOUN _____

VERB _____

ADJECTIVE _____

ADVERB _____

PART OF THE BODY (PLURAL) _____

PLURAL NOUN _____

ADJECTIVE _____

PLURAL NOUN _____

PLURAL NOUN _____

PLURAL NOUN _____

ADJECTIVE _____

NOUN _____

ADJECTIVE _____

PART OF THE BODY _____

MAD LIBS
EXTREME CANNON DODGEBALL

There's a/an _____ new game in town—and its name is
　　　　　　　ADJECTIVE

Extreme Cannon Dodgeball. It's not a thinking _____'s
　　　　　　　　　　　　　　　　　　　　　　　NOUN

game like chess, where it takes a calculated strategy to win or

_____. No, this is a game where you simply need to stay
　　VERB

as alert and _____ as possible and be _____
　　　　　　　ADJECTIVE　　　　　　　　　　　　　　ADVERB

fast on your _____. You duck and dodge to avoid
　　　　　　PART OF THE BODY (PLURAL)

being struck by heavy iron _____ hurtling at you from
　　　　　　　　　　　　　　　PLURAL NOUN

every direction. _____ opposing archers will also shoot
　　　　　　　　　ADJECTIVE

flaming _____ at you. Concentrating is difficult because
　　　　PLURAL NOUN

_____ are crashing all around, and you're constantly
　PLURAL NOUN

trying not to trip over the other _____ on your team. If
　　　　　　　　　　　　　　　　PLURAL NOUN

you manage to catch one of the cannonballs, the _____
　　　　　　　　　　　　　　　　　　　　　　　　ADJECTIVE

gunner who launched it must stand in a penalty _____.
　　　　　　　　　　　　　　　　　　　　　　NOUN

But if you let your _____ guard down for even one
　　　　　　　　　ADJECTIVE

second, you might as well kiss your _____ good-bye!
　　　　　　　　　　　　　　　　　PART OF THE BODY

MAD LIBS® is fun to play with friends, but you can also play it by yourself! To begin with, DO NOT look at the story on the page below. Fill in the blanks on this page with the words called for. Then, using the words you have selected, fill in the blank spaces in the story.

Now you've created your own hilarious MAD LIBS® game!

A FORMIDABLE OP-*PO*-NENT

PLURAL NOUN _____

PART OF THE BODY (PLURAL) _____

ADJECTIVE _____

NOUN _____

PART OF THE BODY (PLURAL) _____

ADJECTIVE _____

PART OF THE BODY _____

ADJECTIVE _____

ARTICLE OF CLOTHING _____

ADJECTIVE _____

SILLY WORD _____

NOUN _____

ADJECTIVE _____

MAD LIBS

A FORMIDABLE OP-*PO*-NENT

As one of Lord Shen's wolf soldiers, I always thought I had

_____ of steel. But I'll be honest: My _____
PLURAL NOUN   PART OF THE BODY (PLURAL)

still shake when I remember my _____ encounter with
                                     ADJECTIVE

the Dragon Warrior. Just thinking about it makes me want to climb

under the nearest _____ and hide. I remember hurrying
                        NOUN

to reload the cannon. Shen had instructed us not to fire until we saw

the whites of the Dragon Warrior's _____. Next
                                     PART OF THE BODY (PLURAL)

thing I knew, there was this blinding flash and the Dragon Warrior

was standing right in front of me, looking all _____
                                                    ADJECTIVE

and ready to kick some wolf _____. I was so
                                 PART OF THE BODY

_____, I almost jumped out of my _____!
ADJECTIVE   ARTICLE OF CLOTHING

I knew what this _____ warrior was capable of. I think
                     ADJECTIVE

I screamed "_____!"—or maybe it was "Mommy!" And
                SILLY WORD

then I did what any respectable _____ would do—I ran
                                     NOUN

for my _____ life!
            ADJECTIVE

From KUNG FU PANDA 2 MAD LIBS® · Kung Fu Panda 2 ™ & © 2011 DreamWorks Animation L.L.C.
Kung Fu Panda ® DreamWorks Animation L.L.C. Published by Price Stern Sloan,
a division of Penguin Group (USA) Inc., 345 Hudson Street, New York, NY 10014.

MAD LIBS® is fun to play with friends, but you can also play it by yourself! To begin with, DO NOT look at the story on the page below. Fill in the blanks on this page with the words called for. Then, using the words you have selected, fill in the blank spaces in the story.

Now you've created your own hilarious MAD LIBS® game!

THE FINAL SHOWDOWN

ADJECTIVE _____

ADJECTIVE _____

PLURAL NOUN _____

NOUN _____

PLURAL NOUN _____

PART OF THE BODY (PLURAL) _____

NOUN _____

ADJECTIVE _____

PLURAL NOUN _____

NOUN _____

PERSON IN ROOM _____

NOUN _____

NOUN _____

ADJECTIVE _____

ADJECTIVE _____

MAD LIBS
THE FINAL SHOWDOWN

Things were not looking _____ for our heroes. The
ADJECTIVE

Furious Five were chained to a/an _____ cannon, and Po
ADJECTIVE

had been blown away by one of Shen's powerful _____.
PLURAL NOUN

Suddenly, a mysterious _____ appeared. Po was back!
NOUN

Shen's army of _____ pounced, but Po used his
PLURAL NOUN

superstrong _____ to blast himself free. He tossed
PART OF THE BODY (PLURAL)

a/an _____ ax so the Five could free themselves. Then
NOUN

the cowardly Shen put _____ citizens in danger as
ADJECTIVE

a diversion. Between battling the _____ and saving
PLURAL NOUN

the citizens, Po's team was fighting a losing _____.
NOUN

Masters Shifu, Ox, and _____ arrived to help, but Shen
PERSON IN ROOM

blasted everyone with a/an _____. Luckily, in the
NOUN

_____ of time, an angry Po was able to summon his
NOUN

Inner Peace and use its _____ power to defeat Shen,
ADJECTIVE

telling him: *You took everything from me, but in the end it only*

made me _____.
ADJECTIVE

MAD LIBS® is fun to play with friends, but you can also play it by yourself! To begin with, DO NOT look at the story on the page below. Fill in the blanks on this page with the words called for. Then, using the words you have selected, fill in the blank spaces in the story.

Now you've created your own hilarious MAD LIBS® game!

A WARRIOR-WORTHY FEAST

ADJECTIVE _____

NOUN _____

PERSON IN ROOM _____

ADJECTIVE _____

NOUN _____

PART OF THE BODY _____

VERB _____

NOUN _____

PLURAL NOUN _____

PLURAL NOUN _____

TYPE OF LIQUID _____

PLURAL NOUN _____

PLURAL NOUN _____

A PLACE _____

ADJECTIVE _____

NOUN _____

PERSON IN ROOM _____

ADJECTIVE _____

ANIMAL (PLURAL) _____

ADJECTIVE _____

Victory sure tastes _____—and so do Mr. Ping's noodles!
ADJECTIVE

To commemorate the _____ Warrior and the Furious
NOUN

Five's triumph over the evil _____, you are invited
PERSON IN ROOM

to attend a/an _____ private party at the Dragon
ADJECTIVE

Warrior Noodles and Tofu restaurant. It will be a celebration fit for

a/an _____! The _____-watering, all-you-
NOUN   PART OF THE BODY

can-_____ buffet meal will include the Dragon Warrior's
VERB

personal favorites: _____ dumplings, tofu-encrusted
NOUN

_____, and noodle _____ a la mode. Bottles
PLURAL NOUN   PLURAL NOUN

of chilled _____ will be cracked open, and we will
TYPE OF LIQUID

raise our _____ in thanks to Po and the Five for once
PLURAL NOUN

again risking their _____ to restore peace to (the)
PLURAL NOUN

_____ and protect its _____ citizens. Live
A PLACE   ADJECTIVE

_____ music will be provided by _____ and
NOUN   PERSON IN ROOM

the _____ _____. We hope you can attend.
ADJECTIVE   ANIMAL (PLURAL)

A/An _____ time will be had by all!
ADJECTIVE

From KUNG FU PANDA 2 MAD LIBS® · Kung Fu Panda 2 ™ & © 2011 DreamWorks Animation L.L.C.
Kung Fu Panda ® DreamWorks Animation L.L.C. Published by Price Stern Sloan,
a division of Penguin Group (USA) Inc., 345 Hudson Street, New York, NY 10014.

This book is published by

PSS!
PRICE STERN SLOAN

whose other splendid titles include
such literary classics as

Best of Mad Libs®	Mad Libs® in Love
Camp Daze Mad Libs®	Mad Libs® on the Road
Christmas Carol Mad Libs®	Mad Mad Mad Mad Mad Libs®
Christmas Fun Mad Libs®	Monster Mad Libs®
Cool Mad Libs®	More Best of Mad Libs®
Dance Mania Mad Libs®	Night of the Living Mad Libs®
Dear Valentine Letters Mad Libs®	Ninjas Mad Libs®
Dinosaur Mad Libs®	Off the Wall Mad Libs®
Diva Girl Mad Libs®	The Original #1 Mad Libs®
Dude, Where's My Mad Libs®	P. S. I Love Mad Libs®
Family Tree Mad Libs®	Peace, Love, and Mad Libs®
Fun in the Sun Mad Libs®	Pirates Mad Libs®
Girls Just Wanna Have Mad Libs®	Prime-Time Mad Libs®
Goofy Mad Libs®	Rock 'n' Roll Mad Libs®
Grab Bag Mad Libs®	Slam Dunk Mad Libs®
Graduation Mad Libs®	Sleepover Party Mad Libs®
Grand Slam Mad Libs®	Son of Mad Libs®
Happily Ever Mad Libs®	Sooper Dooper Mad Libs®
Happy Birthday Mad Libs®	Spooky Mad Libs®
Haunted Mad Libs®	Straight "A" Mad Libs®
Holly, Jolly Mad Libs®	Totally Pink Mad Libs®
Kid Libs Mad Libs®	Upside Down Mad Libs®
Letters from Camp Mad Libs®	Vacation Fun Mad Libs®
Letters to Mom & Dad Mad Libs®	We Wish You a Merry Mad Libs®
Mad About Animals Mad Libs®	Winter Games Mad Libs®
Mad Libs® for President	You've Got Mad Libs®
Mad Libs® from Outer Space	

and many, many more!
Mad Libs® are available wherever books are sold.